The Berenstain Bears' ®
PET SHOW

Stan & Jan
Berenstain

a
BIG
PET SHOW
FOR PETS OF
EVERY SHAPE
AND SIZE!
AND EVERY
PET WILL
WIN A PRIZE!

sourcebooks
jabberwocky

Sister loved
her little fish.
He lived in a bowl,
which sat in a dish.

Sister named her
pet fish Swish,
because when he swam
his tail went *swish*.

When Swish saw food,
he did a perfect figure eight.
The Bears agreed:
Sister's fish was really great.

Brother had
a fine pet, too—
a little bird
named Little Bird Blue.

She was supposed to be
a talking bird,
but she never said
a single word.

CREAK

She made all sorts
of sounds instead,
before and after
she was fed.

She made the sound
of a creaking door.

She made the sound
of a squeaking floor.

She made the sound
of a typewriter clacking.

She made the sound
of a toy duck quacking.

She was a clever
little bird,
though she never said
a single word.

Brother and Sister
said, "Wow! Yippe!"
when they saw a poster
on a tree.

BIG
PET SHOW
FOR PETS OF
EVERY SHAPE
AND SIZE!
AND EVERY
PET WILL
WIN A PRIZE!

"Big pet show!" the poster said.
"For pets of every shape and size!
And every pet will win a prize!"

"Hmm," said Sister,
"how can that be?"
"Don't know," said Brother.
"Let's sign up and see."

The pets, they came
from miles around.
Fred brought Snuff,
his sniffer hound.

When Snuff sniffed
Lizzy Bruin's cat,
Fred said, "Lizzy, look at that!
Snuff made friends with your cat."

Other dogs came,
oodles and oodles:

Dachsies,

Scotties,

Yorkies,

Poodles.

Hunting dogs,

dogs with spots,

a dog with lots
and *lots* of spots.

Were there other cats?

Yes, there were:

A cat with long
and lovely fur.

A cat with kittens
in a box.

A cat on a cushion.

A cat named Socks.

Plus Swish and Brother's
bird, of course.
"Look! Squire Grizzly's
brought his horse!"

"A skunk! A skunk!"
cried the cubs, surprised.

"Do not worry,
my pet skunk's *deodorized*."

PET SHOW

Then Brother Bear
and Sister spied
a sight that opened
their eyes up wide.

JUDGE

A plastic box
is what they saw.
A plastic box
with a soda straw.

"This is my pet,"
said Barry Bear.
But the box was empty!
Nothing was there!

"Look again!
A flea's in there."

"The soda straw's
to give him air."

What a show!

With pets of every sort and size!

But how can each one

win a prize?

You may well wonder
how could that be?
Just turn the page
and you will see.

How about Swish
and Brother's pet?
What sort of prizes
did they get?

Though Little Bird Blue
spoke not a word,
she won the prize
for cleverest bird.

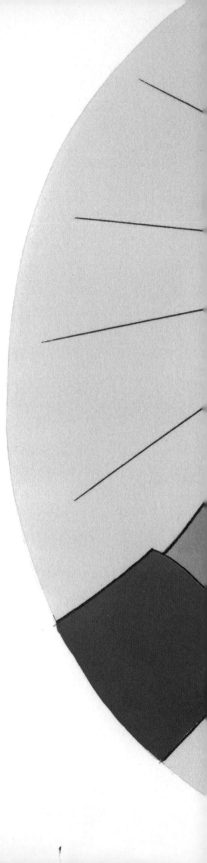

And all agreed
that Swish was great.
His prize said,
"Best Figure Eight."

Published by Sourcebooks Jabberwocky, an imprint of Sourcebooks, Inc.
P.O. Box 4410, Naperville, Illinois 60567-4410
(630) 961-3900
Fax: (630) 961-2168
www.jabberwockykids.com

Originally published in the United States of America by Golden Books.

Library of Congress Cataloging-in-Publication data is on file with the publisher.

Source of Production: Leo Paper, Heshan City, Guangdong Province, China
Date of Production: February 2014
Run Number: 22292

Printed and bound in China
LEO 10 9 8 7 6 5 4 3 2 1